Crocodile!

First published in 2009
by Wayland

This paperback edition published in 2010 by Wayland

Wayland
338 Euston Road
London NW1 3BH

Wayland Australia
Level 17/207 Kent Street
Sydney, NSW 2000

Series Editor: Louise John
Editor: Katie Powell
Cover design: Paul Cherrill
Design: D.R.ink
Consultant: Shirley Bickler

A CIP catalogue record for this book is available from the British Library.

ISBN 9780750257312 (hbk)
ISBN 9780750260275 (pbk)

Printed in China

Wayland is a division of Hachette Children's Books,
an Hachette UK Company

www.hachette.co.uk

Crocodile!

Written by Liss Norton
Illustrated by Emma McCann

Fergus the frog lived in a pond. He was small and green like all the other frogs.

He swam and hopped like all the other frogs.

He ate flies and he croaked like all the other frogs.

But there was something rather special about Fergus.

Whenever there was trouble, Fergus became... Superfrog!

Superfrog was brave and strong. He wore a red suit and a matching red helmet with a yellow stripe. He had red rocket boots so that he could fly.

One day, Superfrog was looping the loop in his rocket boots with his best friend, Doris, when he heard a loud click-clack coming from the ground below.

Fergus and Doris flew down to investigate.

“Yikes!” Doris cried.

A great big, scaly crocodile was hurrying towards the pond. It was click-clacking its sharp teeth at anything that got in its way.

Fergus flew down and landed
in front of the crocodile.
"Who are you?" he demanded.

"I'm Crusty and I've escaped from
the zoo," snapped the crocodile.
"Now get out of my way."

"I bet that pond is full of delicious frogs," Crusty said, and he grinned a mean, toothy crocodile grin.

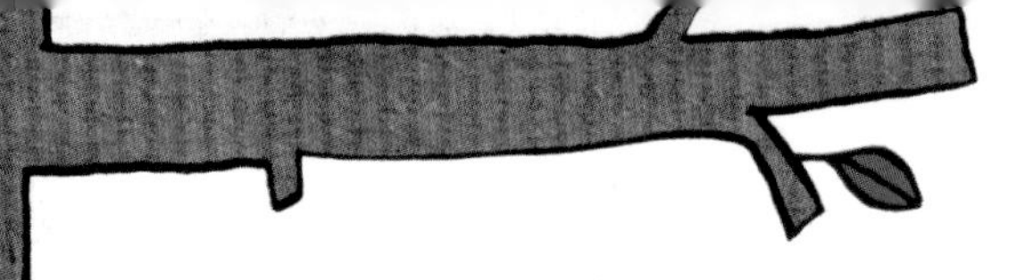

All of Fergus's family and friends lived in that pond. Fergus didn't want them to be gobbled up for lunch!

Fergus looked at the crocodile's sharp teeth. He eyed his strong tail and legs. Crusty was enormous! And Fergus was very small.

"You'll never stop him, Fergus!" said Doris.

But Fergus couldn't let the crocodile eat his family and friends. "If you go any nearer you'll be sorry," he shouted.

Crusty laughed. "Who's going to make me sorry?" he hooted. "You?"

"Yes, me!" Fergus shouted bravely. "And me!" whispered Doris.

Crusty lunged at Fergus and Doris, snapping his sharp teeth at them. Fergus dived out of the way just in time, dragging Doris with him.

Crusty tried again. This time, Fergus quickly leapfrogged over the scaly crocodile. Nothing frightened Superfrog!

Crusty raced towards the pond.
All of Fergus's family and friends
watched in horror.

"Stop him!" shouted Doris.

Just as Crusty was about to dive in, Fergus grabbed his tail and pulled.

"Let go!" Crusty shouted.
But Fergus held on tight to
Crusty's tail. He ducked
underneath his snapping teeth.

Using all of his Superfrog strength, Fergus began to spin Crusty by his tail.

Round and round he flew, getting faster and faster.

"Let go!" Crusty shouted again. "I'm dizzy!"

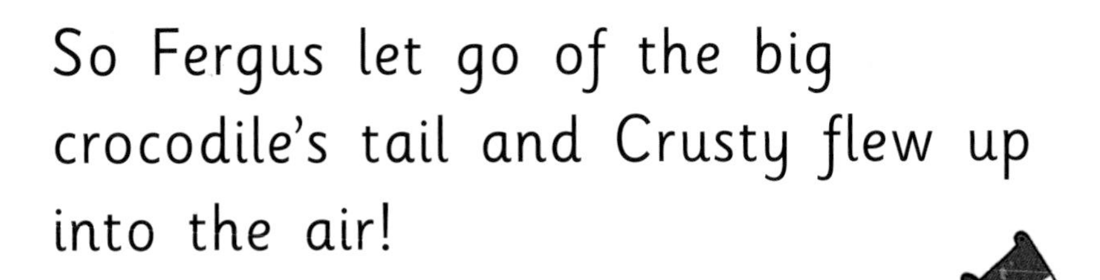

So Fergus let go of the big crocodile's tail and Crusty flew up into the air!

Up, up and up he whizzed.

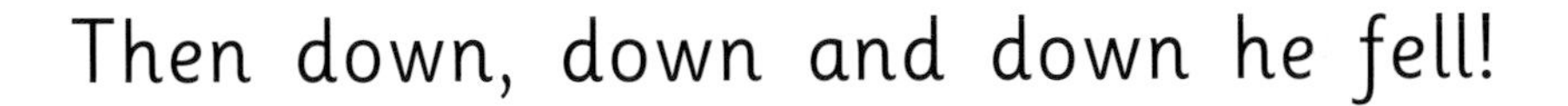

Then down, down and down he fell!

Crusty landed nose-first in a deep muddy puddle. Splat!

He picked himself up and ran back to the zoo as fast as he could.

All of Fergus's family and friends clapped and cheered.

"What a hero!" cried Doris. "Fergus, you've saved the day again!"

START READING is a series of highly enjoyable books for beginner readers. **The books have been carefully graded to match the Book Bands widely used in schools.** This enables readers to be sure they choose books that match their own reading ability.

Look out for the Band colour on the book in our Start Reading logo.

The Bands are:

START READING books can be read independently or shared with an adult. They promote the enjoyment of reading through satisfying stories supported by fun illustrations.

Liss Norton used to be a teacher. She now writes books, musicals and plays for children. She is keen on growing organic fruit and veg at her allotment, on her granddaughters, Maddie and Arabella, and on visiting castles. One day she hopes to find a secret passage...

Emma McCann is currently living a dual life. By day, she is a mild-mannered illustrator, but by night she becomes the masked crime-fighter and master cake-baker "Red Velvet". She hopes to be joined soon in her crime fighting/cake baking adventures by a small, dog-shaped partner.